He Looked at Me

A Fiction About a Real Story

DONNIE TRUE

Paper back ISBN-13: 978-1-946469-44-1
Hardcover ISBN-13: 978-1-946469-47-2

ShelteringTree.Earth, LLC Publishing
PO Box 973, Eagle Lake, FL 33839

Visit our website: ShelteringTree.Earth

Did you enjoy this book?

We love to hear from our readers.

Please email the author through the author page on our website, or write to the author at the address above.

DEDICATION

I dedicate this book to everyone who believes that Jesus Christ is the Son of God. I dedicate it to my parents; Marshall and Jewel, who brought me up in a home full of love; where God, the Bible and Church meant something to them. I dedicate this book to my wife Teresa, who has been my rock for over 40 years and has always loved me no matter what I do or have done. But, most of all, I thank God for His love, mercy and forgiveness.

The historical details of this story are based on

Luke 2, Matthew 2 and 26, and John 18-19.

I always knew what I wanted to be when I grew up. I've known it for as long as I can remember: A Centurion Guard for the King. I remember the first time I saw Gershem. He was the commander for the King's Royal Guard. He had come to Bethlehem several times to get prisoners or just to make a show of force for the King. He was almost a god in my eyes. His armor, his shield, his spear, his helmet, it all was so spectacular that when wearing it, he would catch the eye of anyone he passed. He caught my eye the first time I saw him, and I never felt the same after that day. Yeah, a Centurion Guard. I could never imagine what life would have in store for me.

Of course, as life would have it, my dad had different plans for me. You see, my dad was an Inn Keeper and had been all his life. His business was handed down to him from his father, and so he had the same plan for me. The problem was that I wanted no part of this kind of life, especially if I could become a Centurion Guard. I wanted to be famous like Gershem, not some Inn Keeper. So as fate would have it, my dream came true after several years, and I became what I had always wanted to be. Or did I?

It began when I was a little boy, and all I remember was being awakened every day by my Dad. It was the same routine day after day. "Marcus, he would say, "get up. It's time to feed the animals and clean the stables. Eat a good breakfast son, so you will be strong enough to do your chores." Little did he know that I would eat well and work hard to become someone else.

It was real boring doing my chores, but I did so because I was raised to be obedient to my parents. I just had a different plan for my life than that of my Dad. Of course, doing chores gave me a chance to practice my sword and spear moves. The problem was that a pitchfork and a slat of wood just didn't feel right. But I made them work. I would practice for what seemed like hours or until I heard my father coming to check on me. I didn't want him to see me practicing with my sword and spear. He just wouldn't understand. That was my routine for many days until that one day.

Oh yeah, one more thing before I go on. I always felt like Mom and Dad believed in God, but they just never talked about religion or those kinds of things. They were good parents and helped other people in need on a regular basis, but I really never had a reason to think about or dwell on God. I just grew up in a time where religion was something someone else did. However, here's how it all started.

As I was doing my daily chores on a rather cold day, Dad came into the stables with a man and woman. The woman looked as if she were fixing to have a baby really soon. It was somewhere around the end of the calendar year. I'm not real sure of the date; I just remember that it was very cold, and I couldn't believe that Dad was letting someone spend the night in one of our stables. He told them that he has no more room in his inn and that this stable was the only thing left in town. He told them that we would try to make their stay as pleasant as we could. As luck would have it, I had just finished cleaning the center stall, and it was ready to go. But instead of putting an animal in it we fixed it up for these people. My Dad introduced me to them and told them if they needed anything to call for me. It's funny because after a period of time, I forgot their names. But that's not the most important thing I forgot. I'll tell you that later. They got settled in for the night, and we left them alone.

I would see them each morning and tend to their needs. Boy, was I surprised to find out on the third day the woman, whose name was Mary, had a baby boy. My Mom told me at breakfast that morning about how they had been up almost all night helping to deliver the baby. Mom told me that Mary had done extremely well with childbirth. Mom had helped many of her friends with childbirth before, but she said something was different with this one. She said she just couldn't figure out what it was.

During the days following the baby's birth, the dad, Joseph would leave to take care of something called the census that the Roman Governor had declared has to be done. He would be gone most of the day, and I tried to stay around to help Mary out with the baby. You see, I had a baby brother, and I had to help my mom out sometimes with him, so I kind of knew what to do. Mary and Joseph only stayed for a few weeks after the birth and then had to leave to go back to Jerusalem. It seemed like they were in a hurry to leave, but boy, things got strange before they left.

Right before they were ready to leave, a group of shepherds came to visit them. I was trying to hide so they wouldn't think that I was being nosey. I could see them, and they sure looked excited and happy to see the baby. It was almost like it was the baby that they had come to see and not the parents. I didn't think much about it because I remember how many people came to see Mom and Dad after my little brother was born. The one thing that really surprised me was to see three men show up who were dressed up like some type of Kings or something. And on top of that, I remember that they brought in some gifts that I had never seen before. But they looked very important, so I didn't think any more about it. I just figured that maybe Mary and Joseph must have been someone real important to have those types of visitors. I never realized at the time just how important they really were.

The day that they were ready to leave, Mary called me over to help her pack up her things while Joseph was paying for the stay. I never asked my dad if he gave them a break on the charges because they had to stay in the stables, but I always felt like he did. But my dad did tell me later how proud of me he was for keeping the animals fed and watered because he said he had never had them be so quiet before. I never thought about until later.

When I went over to help Mary, she said, "Marcus, would you like to hold the Baby?" Of course, I did because I had some experience in doing this. I had held my baby brother before. When she handed me the baby, it suddenly hit me that I had never asked anyone what the boy's name was.

So, I said, "I never asked, but what did you name this cute little boy?'

She looked at me and with a great big smile, she said, "Jesus."

I thought what a strange name. I had never heard anyone called this before. But I liked it for some reason.

When I had him in my arms, the funniest thing happened that I remembered at a later date. You see I forgot his name for a long time, but I did remember this. While holding him and talking baby talk to him like I used to do to my brother, he opened his eyes and smiled at me. I tell you; I still remember that it felt like he was looking into my very being. I had never felt like that before when holding other babies. Not even my brother. But his eyes focused on mine, and he clearly smiled at me. I would remember this later on in my life.

Mary, Joseph, and baby Jesus left that day and life went on as usual. I went to school, did my chores, and practiced being a Centurion Guard when Dad wasn't around.

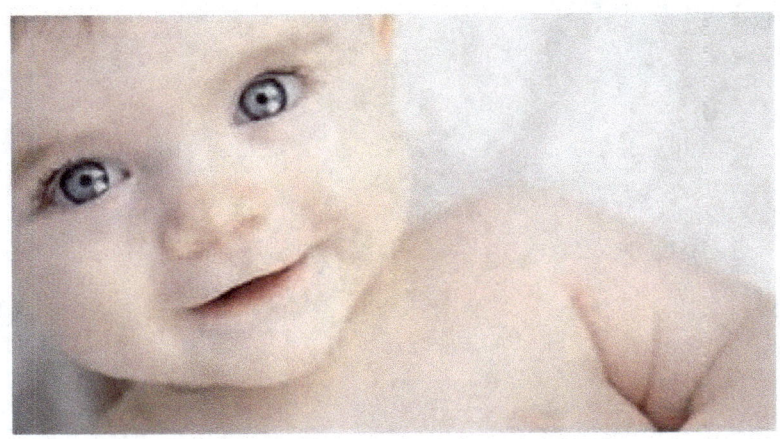

Time passed and I grew up. Eventually, Mom and Dad realized that I didn't want to carry on the business. My dad, being a businessman, had made friends with some of the upper ranking military men and got me into the Royal Guard when I turned 18 years old. That was the starting age for training in the King's army. I trained hard for several years and found favor with the commander of the Centurion Guard. I had become very strong and very adept with my military skills. After all, I had a lot of practice training growing up in the stables.

The problem was that I was becoming just like the Centurion Gershem who I had always wanted to be like. What I mean is that I was tough and hard on prisoners and criminals to the point that I was getting a reputation because of it. I really didn't want to be like that, but I was a Centurion and loyalty to the King and Guard was everything. I had been given my own squad of soldiers to keep order in the surrounding towns and make arrests when ordered to. I would take my prisoners to be jailed in Jerusalem. And sometimes, I'm ashamed to say, I wasn't very nice to them. But I was a soldier, and I had a reputation to keep.

During this time, I married my sweetheart, Rebecca. After a couple of years, we had a son and named him Joshua. I thought my life was great, and I was doing fine as a soldier, dad, and husband. Well at least I thought I was.

I would stop by to see Mom and Dad whenever I had a chance. I was always busy, but I knew they enjoyed the visit from me to see how we all were doing. They began telling me how they had started going to the Temple to worship and how they were learning more about God and things like that. I could see a good change in my parents lives and attitude over time. Dad would always want to talk to me about God, but I just didn't want to get involved. You see I was a Centurion Guard and I had more important things to worry about. I just didn't make that religious stuff a priority for me or my family. After all, I had it all; the power, the respect, and the ability to command others. I had finally become the man that I had always wanted to be.

Little did I know how much my life was about to change.

On the way home from work one day, I noticed a large crowd of people standing around a man who appeared to be teaching something, or perhaps he might have been one of those religious guys going around stirring up trouble. As a soldier, I didn't have much time for religion, and the King always seemed disturbed by them. He didn't have much patience for them at all. Well neither did I. I guess what I'm saying is I didn't spend a lot of time talking about God much less talking to God. I never made time to go and worship at the Temple like the religious people did. I just lived my life like a soldier and took care of my family. And I am ashamed to say, we didn't talk about God very much at home either.

The closer I got to the crowd, I noticed a man who looked very peaceful and heard him talking about the kingdom of God and about loving one another and things like that. The only kingdom I knew about was the King's kingdom. After all, I was doing what I had always wanted to do, be a Centurion guard.

As I stood there for a moment listening, I asked what appeared to be one of his followers, "Who is this man?"

He looked at me in dismay and said, "Why this man is Jesus, Jesus of Nazareth. Haven't you heard of him?"

I did remember that there was a troublemaker going around the country stirring up the people in a religious movement, but I just never dwelt on it.

The man told me that this was Jesus, the king of the Jews, the Savior of the world. He said that he was the King who was born in Bethlehem and the one who had come to set his people free. At that moment, I felt a chill come over me that I could not explain. Then it hit me. He was the baby Jesus that was born in our stable thirty something years ago! I got so excited that I started to shout at him and say "Jesus, Jesus, it's me Marcus, you were born in our stable, remember me?'

With many of his followers looking at me, I suddenly realized that he would not know me. That was many years ago, and he was just a newborn baby when he left. Then just like he had known me all his life, he turned and smiled at me. At that moment I remembered the first time he had looked at me and I how had felt. Now, I was feeling the same way I did many years ago. I felt like he was looking into my very soul. I got nervous and didn't know what to do.

Suddenly, one of the men standing in the crowd said, "You're a Centurion Guard, how do you know Jesus?"

I got all tongue-tied and said, "Oh, I don't, I must have thought he was someone else."

I eased my way back out of the crowd as fast as I could so as not to draw any more attention to myself. What a strange feeling had come over me. I didn't know what to do. This was the man who we had heard about spreading the gospel around for the past several years. We had always heard that he was a troublemaker like the other prophet, John the Baptist, who was beheaded for preaching about God. He got the Scribes and Pharisees mad at him for baptizing people and telling them about someone else who was coming after him who saved them from their sins.

But this man seemed so peaceful. I had heard about him healing the sick, causing the lame to walk and the blind to see, and there were even rumors that he had raised the dead. I didn't know what to think about this; I just knew something about him was real and different.

I hurried to get home so I could tell Rebecca what had just happened. I had never told her about the time that we had a baby born in our stables when I was younger. I couldn't wait to tell her about it now and how I had just seen him again after all these years. What a coincidence. Or was it?

When I got home, I was so excited as I began to tell Rebecca everything. After I had finished telling her the whole story, she told me that she had never seen me that excited before, except when Joshua was born. I told her that just having Jesus look at me had made me feel a way that I had never felt before. I didn't understand what I was feeling. I just knew that something was different. Little did I know what the next few days would bring or how much the events that were about to unfold would change my life forever.

But what a change it would make.

The morning began as it had for the past several years. I would get up early, eat the breakfast that Rebecca had fixed for me and then leave the house before Joshua would get up. The moment I left the house, I knew something was going on. There were people talking beneath their breath and looking scared as if something bad had happened the night before.

As I got to work, I noticed that the other guards were talking about one of the followers of this prophet who had been talking to the High Priests. Evidently, this follower had been paid by the priest to tell them where this prophet was staying. The man whose name was Judas told the priests that this prophet had been telling everyone that he was the son of God. This had made the priests very angry.

When I finally got to my men at work, I found out that we were ordered to go and arrest this troublemaker who had been causing what appeared to be religious problems. We were told to wait for a couple of hours before we made the arrest. My commander wanted us to make sure that this man was where we were we told he would be.

Man, did things start to get out of control. As we arrived at the Garden of Gethsemane with some of the officials from the Chief Priest and Pharisees to make the arrest, this man named Judas would let us know which man was the prophet by kissing him on the check. As we got closer to this place, I realized that the man we were going to arrest was the man named Jesus.

Something just didn't feel right. As we got closer to Jesus, I heard him say something to Judas about being there. And before I knew it, one of the other followers who was trying to protect Jesus pulled out a sword and cut the ear off of Malchus, a servant of the High Priest.

Things were fixing to get ugly when suddenly, Jesus spoke and said for everyone to be calm. I tell you, if I hadn't seen what happened next with my own eyes, I never would have believed it. Jesus reached down to the ground, picked up the soldier's ear and put it back on him like nothing had happened. I testify to you that I saw this for myself. After that, he told his other followers that everything would be alright and to let him go with us. We were told later that the follower who had turned Jesus in to us had committed suicide later that day. That was the least of things that was about to unfold over the next several hours.

We were told to take Jesus to Annas Ben Seth, who was the father-in-law of Caiaphas, the High Priest of the year. Caiaphas was the one who said it would be good if one man died for the people. Inside the courtyard, the High Priest began to question Jesus his about his disciples and what he had been teaching. Jesus replied that what he had been teaching was always in the open, and he never tried to teach anything in secret.

When Jesus told the High Priest that he should not question his teaching but ask the people who had heard him, one of the officials struck him in the face and told Jesus that his reply was very disrespectful.

Jesus replied and said, "Why do you strike me if I tell the truth?"

I became very angry at the way Jesus was being treated. But I could not do anything at this moment because I was a soldier first and had to be careful what I did or what I might say.

After that, we took Jesus to Caiaphas the High Priest.

During this time several people came forward and gave false testimony against Jesus. Caiaphas listened for a short while and then asked Jesus if he was the Son of God. I was really surprised at his answer. His reply was, "Yes, I am." This made the High Priest so mad that he tore his own clothes and accused Jesus of blasphemy.

At that moment, the people around Jesus began to spit at him and began to beat him with their fists. Some of my soldiers joined in. I could not stop them because there were too many people around, but I knew that this was not right.

Early the next morning, which was a Friday, the Sanhedrin - the Council of the Elders of the people and the Chief Priests and teachers of the law -- met before Jesus and questioned him again about who he was. The got really mad with his answers. The Sanhedrin convicted him of blasphemy, which was a death sentence. But Jews couldn't execute anyone, so they had us take him to the Roman Governor, Pontius Pilate.

Pilate found no basis for charges against him because he was not under his authority and told us to take him back to Herod. Herod made fun of Jesus and had some of my soldiers dress him in an elegant robe and sent him back to Pilate. I was getting more and more angry at the way everyone was treating Jesus. I also didn't understand why I was feeling this way.

We finally took Jesus back to Pilate for the last time. Pilate had said that he found no reason to punish Jesus but was afraid of what the crowd might do. Pilate knew that he had the authority to release a prisoner at this time because it was a custom of the Passover.

He asked the crowd if they wanted him to release Jesus. The crowd started shouting, "No, we want Barabbas!" Barabbas was another prisoner we had arrested several days ago. He was a bad man who had been in trouble with the law several times before. I couldn't believe that these people would want to release him instead of Jesus. These were the same people who had been listening to Jesus speak just days before. Jesus had done nothing wrong as far as I knew. Why would these people want to harm Jesus? I just didn't understand.

Pilate then agreed to release Barabbas and had Jesus taken off and flogged by my men. I did not take part in this, but I didn't stop it either. My men made a crown of thorns and put it on Jesus' head. Then they put his own clothes back on him and began to mock him saying, "Hail, King of the Jews!"

Pilate came out one more time and asked the crowd if he should crucify their king.

They replied, "We have only one King, Caesar."

Then Pilate handed Jesus over to me to be taken to a place called the Skull. This was a site upon a hill that overlooked the valley where we took prisoners to be executed.

My soldiers and I took charge of Jesus and began the walk to the Skull. This was the place where criminals were nailed to a cross to be crucified and die. I could hardly contain myself. I just didn't understand why Jesus was being treated this way. I looked at him and saw a man of compassion and goodness.

Why was he being sent to die? What had he done that was so bad that he was condemned to die? All I had ever heard about this man was that he only did good things. He talked about love and God and turning away from sinful things. He wasn't a criminal. He hadn't killed anyone. He wasn't a robber.

Again, I had to be careful what I said and did because I still had orders to follow. I had taken many prisoners to die at the Skull in the past, and it never bothered me before like it did now. What was going on inside of me?

As we began walking to the Skull, I knew that Jesus would never make it to this place of execution by himself. He was taunted, hit, ridiculed and spat upon by everyone around. My own soldiers were beating and cursing him. Oh, I wanted so badly to stop them, but I couldn't; I had orders to follow.

Suddenly, as if a voice had told me, I spotted a man that I knew of from Cyrene standing in the crowd. His name was Simon. I had heard that this man was a man of peace and faith. He was not acting like all the other people. I quickly grabbed him, and without my guards hearing me, asked him to please help Jesus carry his cross. I still had to be careful of my actions because of my position.

Simon carried Jesus' cross all the way to the hill. This walked seemed like it took forever. The longer it took, the more I felt like something as going on in me. I could not stop thinking that what was going on was wrong. I did not know how to handle my feelings, so I just kept walking forward.

When we finally made it to the hill, I just stood still for a moment. It seemed like hours standing there when suddenly one of my men asked me if I was going to give the order to nail this prisoner to the cross.

I couldn't do it. I paused again, and then another one of my soldiers said, "Marcus, you must give the order." I knew that I had to give the order, but in doing so, I knew that it meant that Jesus would be nailed to his cross.

I gave the order.

In all the other executions that I had been a part of, I never had to be one of the guards who actually drove the nails into the prisoner's hands and feet. I sure wasn't going to do it this time. I had never really thought about or realized how cruel this punishment was until now.

I could not look at Jesus as my soldiers nailed his hands and feet. Jesus cried out in pain as I cried out under my own breath. I could not let my men see what they would say was a weakness. I held back my tears the best I could. Why did I feel this way? How did I know in my heart that this was wrong?

As they stood Jesus up on the cross between two other prisoners, I could not make myself look at him. What was happening to me? What was happening to Jesus?

Almost immediately, one of the prisoners who was hung next to Jesus started making fun of him. He asked Jesus, "If you are truly who you say you are, why don't you call on your angels to rescue you?' Even on the cross, he was being mocked.

The prisoner on the other side of Jesus asked, "Would you remember me this day?'

I will never forget what Jesus said. He painfully turned to the man and said, "Today you will be with me in paradise." I wouldn't understand that statement until later.

As my men were gambling for what was left over of his clothes, I knew that I had to look at Jesus. I didn't understand why I felt so compelled to look at him. As I saw him hanging there, I heard him say the words that changed my life forever.

Jesus was in excruciating pain but still managed to look up toward the skies as if he were looking for someone. Then without warning, he looked back down toward the ground. With clear pain and sadness in his voice, he smiled at me and said, "FATHER, FORGIVE THEM, FOR THEY KNOW NOT WHAT THEY DO."

I knew he was talking to me. I felt that same feeling as I had when as a baby, he had looked at me and again in the marketplace. I could not hold my tears any longer. My heart was broken. I finally understood why I was here.

I knew he had forgiven me for not just the past couple of days, but for all my life. At that moment, I understood who he was. You cannot look upon Jesus' face and not know who he is. I wept like a baby. My men were so busy gambling that they never noticed my emotions. I wouldn't have cared if they had.

Moments later, my men began breaking the legs of the prisoners so that they would die quicker. This was the custom of the land because prisoners weren't supposed to die and be left on the cross on the beginning of the Passover weekend. It was very cruel, but that was the way it was.

For the last time, I looked up at Jesus hanging on that cross. He was in so much pain. I couldn't imagine what must be going on in his mind during these final minutes of his life. I knew that it was just a matter of time before my soldiers would come to Jesus to finish their job. Job, what a word.

I realized at that moment that I had finally become the man I had always wanted to be, a Centurion Guard. I had worked all my life to be in this position. A soldier of a king, a man in charge of others and a man who put other to death. What had I done? Who had I become?

In the final minutes, Jesus looked around at the people who were still there watching this tragic event. And then for the last time, he looked at me. Tears fell down my face so hard that I could hardly see him. In that moment, I stood there as tall and proud as any soldier could. You see, I finally knew who he was. He was the Heavenly King.

He looked back up to heaven and cried out, "FATHER, IT IS FINISHED, INTO THY HANDS I COMMIT MY SPIRIT."

And then he died.

Immediately the ground shook; the skies grew dark, and the people began to yell and scream in fear. As we prepared to take Jesus off the cross, I knew. I don't know how I knew, but I knew. There was a calming spirit inside of me that made me know who this man was. I told my men to wait a minute and look upon this man's face.

I said,

"Behold, THIS TRULY WAS THE SON OF GOD."

We took Jesus down from the cross that evening. But it was different this time. He was not like all the others we had executed before. We usually didn't take much care of their bodies or care how we handled them; we just wanted to finish our jobs and get home. Not this time. My men knew from my remarks about Jesus that they had better show some respect for him, and they did. We gave the body to some of his friends that were still there and then left that hill of death.

When we left there that day, I knew that I would never come back to this place. I left there a changed man that day. How could I have not been changed? When Jesus looked down at me from that cross and said that he forgave me, I knew that I would never be the same. And I haven't been. You see, if you truly come to know Jesus, your life will be changed.

Well, the story doesn't end here. In fact, it's just begun. It took me several days to get over what I had witnessed that day. The drama, the way Jesus was treated, his death, and as I soon found out, his resurrection. Oh yeah, I believe it. I knew the guards who were there on duty that night he was buried. They didn't move his body. In fact, one of them told me that no one came and stole his body that night. He later became a believer like me. He said that only God could have taken that body while they were on guard. And again, I knew what he was saying was the truth.

Over the following weeks to come, my wife and son saw a new husband and dad in me. I was different. I told my family everything that had happened that day. They could see a new me, and they liked it. We began to make friends with some other believers. I had to be careful because I knew I would be in serious trouble if my commander found out. I really believe that God was protecting my family and me.

A few weeks later, I was able to leave the guard. My dad was getting older, and I convinced my commander to let me go home to run our family business. He said that because of my years of service and that I had been a faithful and loyal guard that he would let me go. I had served an earthly king well for many years but now I was serving a Heavenly King.

We moved back home, and I began to run the inn. My mom and dad lived there with us, but their health didn't allow them to work much anymore. I'll tell you something funny. I really enjoyed cleaning the stables every day. I'd rather do that than take care of the inn. I think one reason is because my son gets up each morning and helps me. You see, Dad would always send me out there by myself, but I like helping Joshua do the chores each day.

We hadn't been back but a couple of months when Joshua finally asked me one morning why we never put animals in the center stable. He asked me why I always liked to keep that one clean and neat. This was a moment that I had been waiting for. I knew that he was old enough now for me to tell him the whole story about how my life would be changed by what happened in that stable many years ago.

I said, "Joshua, you remember the story that I told you about a baby named Jesus who was born right here?" He is the one that we believe is God's Son, the Messiah. He is the one that your mom and I go to our friends to learn about and to worship." They teach us that He's coming back someday, and I believe that he is. And I just feel like that when he does, he might want to come by and see the place he was born.

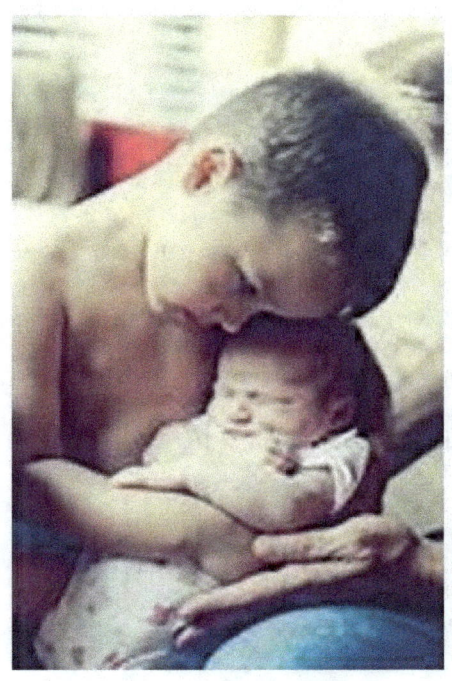

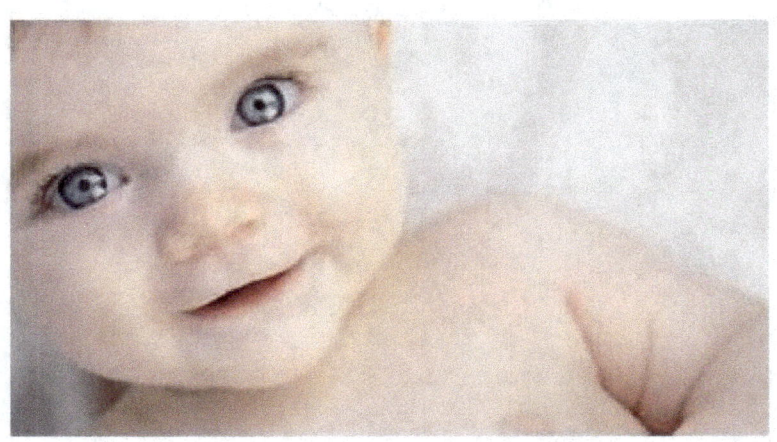

You see Joshua, I just want to be ready for when he does come back. And son, I want you to be ready too. Come here and sit down, Joshua and let me tell you a story about this man named Jesus who smiled at me and how he changed my life.

You see, son, I always knew what I wanted to be when I grew up.

ARE YOU READY?

ABOUT THE AUTHOR

My name is Donald Ray True. I've always gone by the name Donnie. I am a Husband, Father, Son, Grandfather, and Brother. I grew up in a Christian home with Godly parents. I probably asked Jesus into my heart hundreds of times while growing up but finally made it official when I was 27 years old. I have always loved the stories  in the Bible. I taught Sunday School for many years at First Baptist Church in my hometown of Fort Meade. I always wanted to know more about the stories and what happened to many of the people in those stories. I was inspired to write this story because of the centurion at the cross of Jesus who began to shout and sing praises to God after he realized who Jesus was. I wrote this as an inspirational story to get us all thinking about what really happened that day and what happened to the centurion afterwards. I truly believed he was a changed man. I hope you enjoy this story, and it inspires you to read your Bible more.

DISCUSSION GUIDE
for Sunday School classes, Bible study groups,

or personal reflection

1. Why do you suppose Marcus idolized the centurion solder?

2. What kind of compassion, if any, did Marcus' dad have for Mary and Joseph?

_____

_____

_____

_____

_____

_____

_____

_____

3. How do you think Marcus prepared for becoming a centurion while he was growing up?

_____

_____

_____

_____

_____

_____

_____

_____

4. Why would Marcus' dad want him to carry on the family business? Was Marcus expected to do so?

5. What had Marcus heard about this prophet who was getting popular with the people? How did you feel when you starting learning about Jesus?

6. How do you think Markcus felt when he thought Jesus had recognized him in the crowd? Why do you think Marcus denied knowing who Jesus was?

_____

_____

_____

_____

_____

_____

_____

_____

_____

7. What kind of change, if any, did Marcus' family start to see in him after his encounter with Jesus?

_____

_____

_____

_____

_____

_____

_____

_____

_____

8. Why did Marcus struggle with the wayt Jesus was being treated by the people and by his own soldiers?

_____

_____

_____

_____

_____

_____

_____

_____

9. Do you think the soldiers cared about the way they were treating Jesus? Why or why not?

_____

_____

_____

_____

_____

_____

_____

_____

_____

10. Do you think Marcus started second-guessing who he had become? How was this changing his heart?

_____

_____

_____

_____

_____

_____

_____

_____

11. How do you think Jesus can change your heart?

_____

_____

_____

_____

_____

_____

_____

_____

12. In what ways do you think Marcus would become a new man?

13. In what ways has knowing Jesus change you? Or has He?

ABOUT THE ILLUSTRATIONS

When Donnie told me about his story, I knew I was meant to publish it; that's what I do, I find books and stories which I believe God would like to present to the world. However, it was a short story, even though it definitely could stand alone.

I decided that illustrations would be a nice addition. I scoured the internet to find royalty-free images which fit with his story. I used some singularly and others, I made into collages. Some of the images are world-reknown (like the Judas Kiss, the pictures of the tortured Jesus, and Jesus teaching His disciples). The little boy with the wooden sword and the M on his shield was perfect to depict Marcus. The pen and ink Jesus on the cross inspired me to use only black and white, but that fell to the wayside when I found pictures with such rich and emotional colors, I just had to include them.

It is my hope that these illustrations add to Donnie's story and enrich any discussions that might arise from reading and sharing his book.

Most importantly, I hope these illustrations help you understand the love God has for you and the plans He has for you.

In Good Faith,
Evelyn Rainey, Publisher

SHELTERING TREE
EARTH PUBLISHING

Our books will help you feed His sheep.

We are an exclusive publishing house.
Our readers, once they finish one of our books, will be
able to get up and face the world wiser, stronger,
centered, and with the assurance that we are not alone:
we are all a part of the Sheltering Tree on Earth.
If you as a writer feel that same calling, please refer to

https://ShelteringTree.Earth